Wit

8 6494

D0422813

WELCOME TO
PASSPORT TO READING
A beginning reader's ticket to a brand-new world!

Every book in this program is designed to build read-along and read-alone skills, level by level, through engaging and enriching stories. As the reader turns each page, he or she will become more confident with new vocabulary, sight words, and comprehension.

These PASSPORT TO READING levels will help you choose the perfect book for every reader.

READING TOGETHER
Read short words in simple sentence structures together to begin a reader's journey.

READING OUT LOUD
Encourage developing readers to sound out words in more complex stories with simple vocabulary.

READING INDEPENDENTLY
Newly independent readers gain confidence reading more complex sentences with higher word counts.

READY TO READ MORE
Readers prepare for chapter books with fewer illustrations and longer paragraphs.

This book features sight words from the educator-supported Dolch Sight Word List. Readers will become more familiar with these commonly used vocabulary words, increasing reading speed and fluency.

For more information, please visit www.passporttoreadingbooks.com, where each reader can add stamps to a personalized passport while traveling through story after story!

Enjoy the journey!

Little, Brown and Company

Hachette Book Group
237 Park Avenue, New York, NY 10017
Visit our website at www.lb-kids.com

Little, Brown and Company is a division of Hachette Book Group, Inc.
The Little, Brown name and logo are trademarks of Hachette Book Group, Inc.

The publisher is not responsible for websites (or their content) that are not owned by the publisher.

First Edition: April 2012

ISBN 978-0-316-18317-8

10 9 8 7 6 5 4 3 2 1

CW

Printed in the United States of America

Miss Piggy in the Spotlight

by Lucy Rosen
illustrated by Kory Heinzen

LITTLE, BROWN AND COMPANY
Boston   New York

Hi, Muppet fans!

Can you find these things in this book?

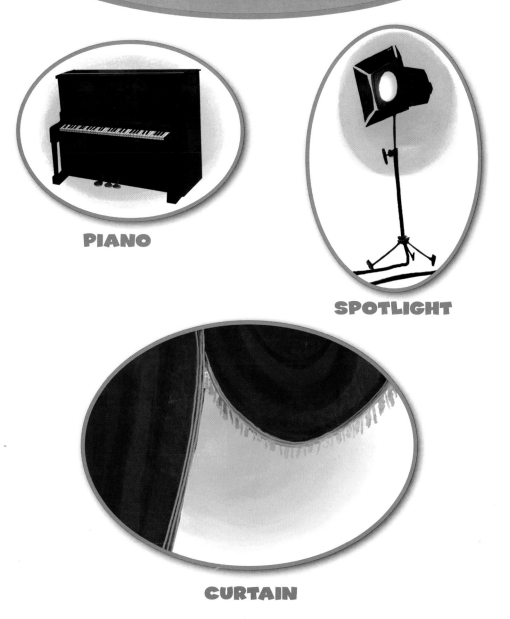

PIANO

SPOTLIGHT

CURTAIN

Backstage at the Muppet Theater
the Muppets were very busy.
In just a few hours,
they would be putting on
one of their biggest shows ever!
Fozzie was practicing his jokes.
Gonzo was giving a pep talk to his chickens.

And Miss Piggy was rehearsing her song,
"All You Need Is *Moi*."
It was going to be the big finish for the show.

"Just a second, Miss Piggy," Kermit said,

interrupting the song.

The frog walked out to center stage.

"Attention, please!

Gather around, everybody!"

"I have great news," Kermit said.
"I have something that will make
this show even more spectacular!"
"Fabulous! You must be adding another
spectacular song for *moi*!" said Piggy.

"Uh...no," said Kermit.

"But I do have a big surprise!

Tonight, you will be onstage with a big star!"

"A star?" asked Rowlf.

"You mean to share the spotlight?"

"Exactly," said Kermit.

"And trust me, this star will shine!"

"Did you hear that?" Fozzie asked

after Kermit left the stage.

"A big star!"

"I wonder if they will go on

 after your act, Miss Piggy," said Rowlf.

"What do you mean?" said Piggy.
"Everyone knows that *moi* sings
the most important song in the show.
And that the most important song is
the *last* song."
"Well, sure," said Rowlf.
"But that was before Kermit called in
someone of note." He plunked on his piano.

13

"Do not be silly," huffed Miss Piggy.

"Kermit would never replace me!"

"If you say so," said Rowlf.

"But do not come howling to me

if this new star takes your place!"

"Big star! Big star!" shouted Animal.

"Get back to work!" yelled Miss Piggy.
"I am the biggest star, and I have a song
to rehearse."

Miss Piggy tried to practice singing,

but she was too worried.

"Take five!" she called for a break.

Then Piggy said quietly to herself,

"No one can take my place, right?"

"Sure they can!" Gonzo piped up.
"Just move over to your left a bit.
I can take your place right now!"

Miss Piggy did not think
what Gonzo said was funny.
"Take that!" she cried.
She grabbed Gonzo by the nose
and pitched him into the balcony.

"Thanks," said Gonzo.

Being a daredevil, Gonzo enjoyed the trip.

"Let that be a lesson
to the rest of you turkeys!" said Miss Piggy.

"Those are not turkeys—
they are chickens!" Gonzo corrected her.

Miss Piggy stormed away.

"Boy, is she in a *fowl* mood!" Gonzo muttered.

Miss Piggy marched backstage
to find Scooter.
He always knew what was going on.
"Oh, Scooter," Miss Piggy said sweetly.
"What can you tell me about this new star
Kermit told us about?"

"Oh," said Scooter, "the new star
is going to be dazzling!"

"More dazzling than... *moi*?" Piggy gasped.

"Absolutely!" Scooter said, nodding his head.

"It cannot be," wailed Miss Piggy.

"Kermit is my one and only.

How could he do this to me?

He could not ask me to share the spotlight

with another star."

"But he is!" said Scooter.

Miss Piggy frowned.

Miss Piggy fumed.

She got mad...very mad...

so mad that the other Muppets

took a step back.

"WHERE IS THAT FROG?" she yelled.

"It is time to get to the bottom of this."

Miss Piggy found Kermit

opening a big box behind the main curtain.

"Listen up, frog," cried Piggy.

"I am going to ask you once, and only once.
Is that star going to upstage *my* big number
tonight?"

"Well, yes, Piggy," said Kermit, "but—"

"THAT IS IT!" screamed Miss Piggy.
"I cannot take it anymore!
How can you do this to me
after all I have done for you
and these weirdos?"

"Wait, Piggy!" said Kermit. "Please!"

"Take THIS," yelled Miss Piggy.

"Hiiiiiiii-yaaaa!"

With one well-aimed swing of her arm,

Miss Piggy karate-chopped Kermit!

"Miss Piggy, you do not understand,"
cried Kermit. "Look inside that box!"
Miss Piggy did not want to do what
Kermit asked.
But after huffing and puffing,
she decided to take a tiny peek inside the box.
She tore away at it piece by piece.
Finally, all that was left was...

"Big star! Big star!" shouted Animal.
Kermit had brought in a huge,
glittering, golden star
to hang in the spotlight
during Piggy's performance.

"Oh, Kermie," said Miss Piggy.

"Is this all for me?"

"Yes," said a dazed Kermit.

"I wanted something to help you shine even more than usual."

"Oh, Kermie!" said Miss Piggy.
She covered Kermit with smooches.
"I should have known you
would never replace me."

"But next time you bring in a star," said Piggy, "you had better clear it with me first!"